Arkansas Stories
Charlie May Simon

Collected, Edited and Introduced
by Lyman B. Hagen, Ph.D.
Arkansas State University

Illustrations by
Susan O'Reilly

AUGUST HOUSE/*Little Rock*

L. R., ARK.

This publication was made possible, in part, by the Jonesboro, Arkansas Literary Club and a grant from the Arkansas Endowment for the Humanities.

Published 1981 by August House, Inc., Publishers, 1010 West Third Street   Little Rock, Arkansas 72201 501-376-4516.

First Edition, September 1981

Library of Congress Catalog Card Number: 81-65366.

Simon, Charlie May
Arkansas Stories

Little Rock, AR: August House

"The Road to St. Charles" was originally published in the May, 1943 issue of *Story Parade*. "New Friends" was first published in the April, 1943, issue of *Child Life*. "The Geography Lesson", "The Song", "The Week of the Fair", and "Buttons" were originally published in *Trails for Juniors*.

Special thanks to Ms. Margaret Arnold and Ms. Elizabeth Smith for their assistance with proofreading and to Mr. Bob Crane for his work as production artist.

ISBN (paperbound) 0-935304-47-9
ISBN (clothbound) 0-935304-22-3

This book, a part of Charlie May Simon's real life, now ended, is dedicated to the children who read it. Through their imagination, they make it real again.

Ted Parkhurst
Managing Writer, August House, Inc.
June 24, 1981

Arkansas Stories

Charlie May Simon was one of the most energetic of Arkansas children's authors. She left for us a rather large body of books and short stories. Simon toured the world pursuing subjects and scenes, but she frequently found her material right at home in folkways of Arkansas to which she was born and always returned.

Many of these stories have long languished out of print in her papers stored at the special collections library of the University of Arkansas at Little Rock. While scanning this material for biographical data, it occurred to me that today's Arkansas children should have the privilege of meeting the words of Charlie May Simon, particularly those concerned with Arkansas locales. Hence, this volume contains six of her tales that evolved from events she observed in her native state.

Charlie May Simon was an astute observer of humankind and painstakingly created her tales. She should remain a source of pride and inspiration to the literary heritage of Arkansas.

Dr. Lyman B. Hagen, Ph.D.
Arkansas State University
February, 1981

Table of Contents

Buttons

The green and white rowboat "Boranders" drifted down with the current so slowly that it made scarcely a ripple on the waves. Donie Lee, with her jeans rolled high above her knees, kicked aside a pile of mussels to make room for her feet, and settled herself more comfortably at the stern.

Tom Lee, her father, sat at the prow, with his face half-turned from her, guiding the boat now and then with an oar. He was a man of few words, but there was a contentment even in his silence. They had had an unusually good day, with the mussels grabbing at the hooks almost as fast as they could let down the lines. Now the boat was so full it could hold no more and they were heading home, with the lines dangling in rows from the iron bars which hung suspended high on each side.

Donie looked idly at the familiar landmarks she passed. There was the tall sweetgum tree growing so close to the river bank that its roots could be seen, like giant black fingers clutching the earth to hold on. The leaves had already turned scarlet and the little starry balls had fallen, bobbing up and down on the waves. A tall blue crane stood on one leg beside it, but he ran awkwardly away at their approach. But two mallards, the first of the season to come down from the north, floated undisturbed in a quiet cove, knowing full well they were safe until hunting season started.

September had always been the month that Donie liked best of the whole year. The days were just right, neither too hot nor too cold. All of nature seemed to be waking up from the drowsiness of summer, with squirrels burying pecans and hickory nuts as fast as they could find them, and rabbits patching up their burrows. Summer birds were fluttering about, getting ready to fly south as the winter birds began coming in. Even the fish seemed to know the seasons were changing, for their runs in the river were as crowded as the flyways of the air.

But now September meant something else, and the thought kept coming back to Donie's mind to nag her. There was a new consolidated school at Riceville, and it took in the settlement of Horseshoe Bend. And the little one-room school where she had been going had been torn down.

It was said of Donie's mother and her people that they never knew a stranger, which meant they could make friends as soon as they met a newcomer, talking and laughing with them as if they'd known each other all their lives. But Donie was like her father. She was more at ease on the river than with people, unless she knew them very well. And there wasn't one in her class that she knew. She could feel their stares and sometimes she wondered if they were not laughing behind her back.

At a clearing around the bend, where a rice field came down to meet the river, two girls were playing. They had taken off their shoes and socks and were holding their crisp starched dresses high, to wade cautiously in the water. They stared at Donie and her father floating past in the "Boranders" and Donie lowered her eyes shyly. She had recognized one as a girl named Ella, in her class at school. Suddenly a loud scream caused her to look up quickly.

"An alligator!" one of the girls exclaimed.

"Oh! He's coming after us!" the other cried.

Donie could see nothing but a gar, with its long, pointed face showing through the muddy water. But the girls were already scurrying away as fast as they could, with their shoes and socks dangling in their hands.

Now it was Donie who stared as they ran through the field of ripe rice to a house high on a hill. How could anybody be afraid of a garfish? Many a time, when she was swimming in deep water, she had come across even larger ones than that, but she hadn't given them a second thought. There was nothing about the river to be afraid of, Donie mused. Even in flood time with the water rising high over the banks, or when a strong wind blew shaking and rocking their houseboat as a terrier shakes a rat, she was never frightened.

There was only one fear that Donie had. The very thought of the room full of strangers she must face again on Monday morning filled her with dread. All week she had looked forward to Saturday when she could go out on the river with her father. And now that Saturday was here, she could not get that dread out of her mind. It had been different at the old school where she had always gone before. There were only the few children that she knew so well, who lived on the river as she did. And they were all in one room, from the first grade to the last.

"Seems like I hear somebody playing a mouth harp," Donie father spoke at last when they came within sight of the houseboat where they lived.

"Uncle Allan!" Donie exclaimed, forgetting her fear for the moment. No one else could play such gay, lively tunes as her mother's brother. "It couldn't be anybody but Uncle Allan!"

He was a sailor, and once a year he came back on a furlough to visit them with his songs and music and his wild tales of adventure.

He came out on the porch of the houseboat when he heard the splash of the oars, and he caught the rope Donie's father threw to make fast the "Boranders."

"Well, Tom, I see you've got yourself a helper," he said, pretending not to recognize Donie in her jeans. "Who is this young fellow anyway?"

"She's about as good a fisherman as there is on the river, I reckon," Tom Lee answered with a slow smile.

"And she's so much a part of the river, I vow I believe the fish all know her," Donie's mother laughed as she came out to greet them. "And the mussels too, I'm bound," she added when she saw how full the boat was.

A tin-bottomed wooden tub, filled with water, was already simmering over an open fire on the river bank. Uncle Allan joined them as they worked in the shade of a drooping willow. His sailor collar and wide-bottomed trousers flapped with each step he took. The mussels were thrown in the hot water to make them open easily, then they were cleaned and put in piles.

"Look, I found a pearl," Donie teased. "It's nothing but a slug. A pearl is round and smooth and full of pretty colors."

"You call that a slug? Why, that's as fine a pearl as ever I saw," he answered, holding it up between his fingers. "That is, except that black pearl I found off the coast of old Mexico."

Uncle Allan had a way of spinning yarns with such a straight face that Donie found herself half believing them even though she knew they couldn't possibly be true. She could almost see the man-eating octopus guarding the bed of giant oysters, each with a priceless pearl inside, as she listened while she worked.

The mussels were assorted into separate piles, and on Monday the shell boat was coming to take them up the river to the button factory. The pile of small yellow sand shells was larger than usual this time. They were used to make the dainty, pearl-like buttons on fine blouses and babies' dresses. The elephant ears, big and black with purple insides, were the cheapest, for they made buttons for under-wear and playsuits. But they were the easiest to catch on the hooks that dragged the river bottom. All the grandma shells and creepers were put in a pile to-gether to be thrown back into the river, for they were of no use in making buttons.

They finished just as the sun went down, with a splash of color on the treetops across the river, and Donie's mother started up the stage board of the houseboat to prepare their supper.

"What will it be," she asked, "venison, bear meat, pork, fish or chicken?"

It was a game they played whenever they had fried turtle, for each part of a turtle has the flavor of some kind of meat.

"Chicken," Donie replied.

"The wishbone for me," Uncle Allan joined in.

It meant that they would have meat from the turtle neck for that was the part that tasted like white meat of a chicken.

Donie took a bath from the back side of the boat and put on a clean shirt and jeans. Cool and re-freshed, she sat down on the bank with her knees drawn up and looked out on the river. The sky was gray, with the first star of the evening appearing above a tall sycamore on the other shore. There was that silence that comes in the pause between the bird songs of the day and the cry of the tree toads and crickets and the chuck-will's widows. Now and then a river swallow, flying back to its nest in the banks, skimmed the water slant-wise, tipping it with a wing. Or, a water snake passed silently by, with its head held high like a prow of a toy boat.

"I wish it could be like this always and always,"

Donie sighed as her uncle came and sat down beside her.

"It seems to me like it is," he said. "It was like this last year when I came and the year before — the houseboats tied to trees on the bank, the mussels in piles and the old muddy river running by. I don't see anything that's changed except the way you've been growing like all get-out. Why, you sprout up another six inches every time I see you."

"If I just didn't have to go to school," Donie answered.

"Oh, so that's what's bothering you," Uncle Allan laughed. "You've had enough learning, you think."

It wasn't because she had had enough of learning. There were still so many things Donie wanted to know besides how to read and write and add. How far was it from here to the evening star, and what went into making the boulder on the opposite shore, and what it was like in all the places where the river ran, from the first little spring up north to the ocean it empties into. But Uncle Allan would never understand what it was to be shy with strangers and to stumble over a lesson just because it had to be recited aloud.

"I knew everybody in the school here at Horseshoe Bend," Donie said. "But there's not a soul in my class at Riceville that's my friend. It's true!"

She half expected her uncle to laugh at her, but instead he answered, slowly, "Yes, I know how it is . . ."

"There wasn't a more bashful boy in the whole school than I was," he went on. "And it was even

18

worse in the Navy when I first went in. Why, I'd sit off in a corner by myself while all the other fellows were having fun, singing and talking and pranking, and none of them paying any attention to me. That is, not until I found the lynx eye. Of course, everything changed after that."

"The lynx eye? What is that?" Donie wanted to know.

"It's something that came from some heathen idol, I was told. It was at a strange port with a name I don't remember, where we'd put in after a long voyage."

All of Uncle Allan's yarns began that way, and Donie found herself listening, as she always did, half believing though she knew it could not possibly be true. She tried to picture her uncle, lonely and shy, with all the other sailors leaving him to go ashore. And the wizened old medicine man rowing out to the ship, trading a magic lynx eye for a pouch of tobacco.

"Where is it?" Donie asked when her uncle had finished his tale.

He hesitated, then shook his head. "I'm not sure I ought to let you see it," he said. "I can see right now you don't believe me. Why, you might even call it a plain old button, for it does look something like one. And could you imagine a lynx eye working magic after that!"

Donie coaxed and at last he went back to the houseboat where he kept his duffel bag. He brought something back in his hand and when he gave it to Donie, she laughed aloud. It was nothing but a plain old button.

"I knew that's what you'd think of it," he said with a frown as he took it back. "Of course, those holes make it look like a button, but they're to put a string through, so it can be worn like this."

He took a string from his pocket and threaded it through one of the holes, then he tied it around Donie's neck.

"I'll bet a silver dollar it would work the magic if you'd wear it to school on Monday," he said. "All you have to do is look straight at the first girl you see in the classroom and smile at her like this," he smiled down at Donie in such a warm, friendly way that she could almost believe what he said was true. "And you say 'hello,' like this. Then watch them come swarming around you like bees after clover. Why, you should have seen how it was when the fellows came back from shore leave, right after I'd got it from the medicine man. It was 'Hi there, Allan.' 'Why didn't you come with us, boy?' You'd think I'd been their pal all my life."

"Supper's ready," Donie's mother called. "And whatever tall tale that is you're telling now will have to wait, Allan."

But Uncle Allan said nothing more about the magic lynx eye until Monday morning when Donie was ready to go to school.

"Now don't forget to wear the magic eye." he whispered. And when he saw it tied around Donie's neck he added. "And mind you, you've got to believe it, or it won't work for you. Remember, just smile, like this."

His smile followed Donie to the road where she waited for the school bus. When she got on the bus the first person she saw was Ella, the girl who lived

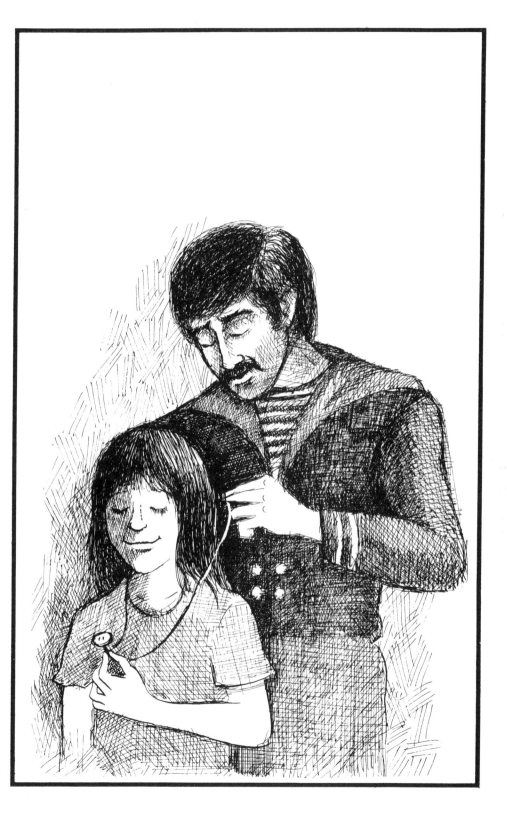

on the rice farm. Donie's cheeks burned at first, and she started to turn shyly away. But she felt the lynx eye cool and firm beneath the neck of her dress and she turned back to Ella smiling the way Uncle Allan had told her, and she said "hello" as he had said it.

Ella looked surprised, then she smiled back and made room on the seat beside her.

"You live on a houseboat, don't you?" she said. "That must be lots of fun."

"It is," Donie answered.

She found herself talking about fishing and swimming and rowing on the river as easily as if they had been friends all their lives. They walked into the classroom arm in arm and when the others in the class turned to look at her, Donie smiled at them. She felt the warmth of friendship all around her, drawing her in as part of them. Even the teacher was not stern as Donie had once thought her to be. And when it was time to recite her lesson aloud, Donie did not once stumble. Could it really be that this button around her neck was a magic eye after all? She must tell Uncle Allan about it as soon as she reached home.

"Mercy, child, what's come over you?" her mother said, looking up from her sewing when Donie came rushing up the stage plank late that afternoon.

"Where's Uncle Allan? I've something to tell him."

"Well, I've something to tell him, too," the mother answered as she rolled up a pair of socks she had mended. It was she who spoke first when Uncle Allan came out on the porch, fresh from a swim in the river. "I thought you had to learn something about keeping socks darned and buttons sewed on in the Navy," she said. "Here, I've finished all your socks, and they were peppered with holes, all right. But your pea jacket — there's a button missing and I can't find it high or low in that duffel bag of yours."

She held up the jacket, and Donie gave a little gasp. There were the remaining buttons, exactly like the magic lynx eye her uncle had given her, and one of them was missing. An embarrassed grin came over Uncle Allan's face and he caught her eye and winked. Donie winked back.

"Here it is." She untied the string and took it off. She didn't need it now, for she knew that the friends she had made that day would still be her friends tomorrow and all the days after.

The Road to St. Charles

"ALL ABOARD," the bus man called.

Mark leaned out the window and called good-by to his father, standing at the station in his trim khaki uniform. Soon he would be leaving, too, for ports far away on tropical islands or in the far north.

"All aboard for Forest City, Brinkley, Clarendon and Duvalls Bluff," the bus man called again.

These were the places where Mark would go, passing through each town on swift wheels until he came to St. Charles, where his Great-Aunt Mary lived. It was there he would make his home until his father returned. What was she like, this Great-Aunt Mary, he wondered. He had not seen her since he was very young, when his father took him there on a visit. Far back in his memory he searched, and there came to his mind a little old woman who didn't like children and who scolded when he made a noise.

It was not too late, even now. He could get off before the bus started, and run back to the town he knew, back to the houses where the people he knew were living. But when he looked out the window, he saw his father still standing there. He would be going, too, to places he did not know, with people strange to him, to fight and lick the enemy.

"I'll be seeing you, Dad," he called out the window.

"Sure thing," his father replied.

The motor started, and slowly the bus pulled out of the station. Away they went, out of the city and across the big river, then along the lonesome highways, speeding to the towns that the bus man called. A steady rain fell, beating down against the window and on the windshield.

"Never saw the river so high since the flood of '27," the man next to Mark said, as if he were speaking to no one in particular. He was a farmer, dressed in blue overalls and jumper, and he held a bag of peanuts in his hands, taking one out now and then and crunching its shell.

"Where are you going, son?" he asked Mark.

"I'm going to St. Charles," Mark replied. "I'm going to live with my great-aunt there while my father is in the Army."

"I live near St. Charles," the man went on, cracking another peanut in his hand. "Out in the country on a rice farm. What's she like, this great-aunt in St. Charles. Maybe I know her."

But Mark could only give her name. And he looked up at the man, waiting to hear what he would say about this great-aunt he did not know.

"Miss Mary Holden," the man repeated, slowly. "No, don't know as I ever heard of her. But there are a lot of people I don't know in St. Charles."

The bus stopped and a woman with three small children got on. Rain dripped from their faces, down over their shoulders, and formed little puddles at their feet.

On both sides of the window could be seen the flat cotton fields, where last year's brown stalks bowed low in the rain, showing now and then a gray, bedraggled boll that had not been picked. They crossed another river and the water ran fast and furious, rising close to the floor of the bridge.

At the next stop, a tall, thin woman got on, with a little gray kitten in a box. The kitten stretched its head out of a hole in the box, and looked around, meowing and purring at the same time. Mark reached over and stroked the kitten, and dimly he remembered an old woman who didn't like cats, and screamed when one came near. Could it have been his Great-Aunt Mary?

They turned off the main highway and on to a gravel road that crept through a swampy forest. Here the river had left its banks and crept over the lowlands, with muddy little waves beating against the tree trunks and over the fallen leaves and twigs. The rain stopped, as if all the water had been drained from the sky, and the sun came out just before it set in the west.

Suddenly the bus came to a stop, and there,

before them, was a sign which read, "Bridge Washed Out."

"That means I'll have to turn around and go back to Clarendon, to cross the river," the bus driver called out.

Clarendon was twenty miles back, Mark knew, for he had been watching the sign posts along the way.

"How far is it from here to St. Charles?" he asked.

"St. Charles is just a mile down the road and across the river," the bus man replied.

"I was never one to turn back when I'm so near to where I'm going," the farmer declared, and he got out of the bus, still eating peanuts from a bag.

Mark followed him, for surely he could get across the river somehow, without going so far back. Then the woman with the cat in the box got out, and behind her came the woman with the three children.

"I live only the next town away, and I won't go back twenty miles to get to it," the lady with the cat remarked.

"I live still farther away," the mother of the three children said, "but I thought this was as far as the bus would go."

The bus was now out of sight, and there was nothing for her to do but walk along the gravel road that led through the swamps, with the others.

Twilight came. A hoot owl called in the forest and the wind whined through the trees with an answering sound. The noise of the rushing river was loud in their ears.

"Is there somebody else behind us?" Mark

asked, for he was sure he heard soft footsteps coming close.

"No, we are all right here," the farmer replied, "But that sounds like footsteps to me, too."

They stopped to listen, but all was still. Then they started on, and the sounds of the footsteps fell softly behind them.

Across the river the lights of St. Charles shone. It seemed so near, this little town where each twinkling light meant a window in some home or store. It seemed to Mark that he could take only a few steps, and there he would be, in one of the lighted rooms, where a warm fire burned. But between him and the town was a raging river.

He walked to the river where nothing showed but the metal braces overhead. Water covered the bridge, sweeping logs and lumber across it as a housewife sweeps chips with her broom.

"There's nothing to do but wait here till morning," the farmer announced.

"I'll get some twigs and we can make a fire," Mark said.

He pulled branches from a dead pine that had been struck by lightning long ago, and the farmer piled them up on the deserted road and lit them. In the firelight, Mark could see the faces of those around him, the farmer in the blue jeans, the tall, thin woman with her three tow-headed children. All else was darkness, made blacker than ever behind the red glow of the fire. The stealthy footsteps that had followed them were silent now.

"I'm hungry," one of the three children said.

"I want some more candy," another chimed in.

"I haven't any candy, but I've fried chicken and

baked ham and buttered biscuits enough for us all," the mother replied.

"I have two chocolate bars," Mark said, and he took them out of his pocket and broke them in small pieces so there would be enough to go around.

The farmer brought out another bag of peanuts and the woman with the cat had a box of candy. By the light of the fire they ate their supper, giving the scraps to the cat in the box. And the farmer told tales of the wild animals of the woods.

"Now that could have been a panther following behind us, for panthers have as much curiosity about folks as cats have," he said. "More than once a man walking in the woods has heard just such footsteps behind him, and never could he see the animal; but when he went back in the daylight, there would be the animal's footprints in the dirt as plain as his own."

"A wildcat will do the same, and so will a fox," the mother of the three children said. She was a country woman and knew the ways of the forest creatures.

There was a rustle of leaves in the darkness behind them, and the sound of breaking twigs. Mark looked around quickly and saw something yellow darting behind a tree.

"That's no panther or wildcat. That's a yellow dog."

He called and held out a piece of ham and biscuit, and slowly the animal came to him. It snatched the food and ran away, but came back again, as if wanting to trust him. Mark gave him his share of the chocolate bar, and the dog ate it. Its tail wagged, slowly at first, then contentedly, as it lay down beside Mark and slept in the warmth of the fire.

The stars climbed high in the sky and the dipper swung over the north star. Never had Mark seen the stars in this place before, for he had always been asleep while Orion was still low on the horizon. One by one the three children put their heads in their mother's ample lap, and fell asleep. Then Mark curled up close to the fire, away from the wind so the smoke would not blow over him, and the dog moved beside him. Did he remember an old woman who hated dogs, too, Mark wondered. Then he yawned and blinked his eyes, and knew nothing more until the orange and gold slants of sunlight came through the forest to shine on him.

The white houses and green lawns of St. Charles could be seen across the river, but it seemed farther away in the light of day, for the river stretched brown and forbidding before them.

"If we had gone back by way of Clarendon, we'd have been there long before now," the woman with the cat remarked.

But nothing could be done about that, now.

The dog raised his head and sniffed, then he ran ahead, and Mark followed to see where he led. Down at the river bank an old coon stood by the water's edge, waiting for a frog or a fish, and when the dog came near, it went dashing up a tree. But also, down at the river bank, an old barge was tied with a stout rope to a tree.

"We'll float across on the barge," Mark called.

"Maybe," the farmer replied. "But it will take a lot of poling to do it."

He searched through the forest and found four

34

strong sapling poles for himself and Mark and the two women. Then they stepped on the barge and as soon as the rope was untied, they paddled the water as hard as they could.

"Go up the river and pole hard while you're doing it," the farmer said.

"But St. Charles is back the other way," Mark objected.

"Never mind, these waves will get you to St. Charles all right."

The water lapped at the barge, and pushed against it, trying to take it down stream as it did the logs and fallen trees, and the barge rocked and swayed, but it landed safely at last, on the other side of the river.

Down the streets of St. Charles they walked, with their bundles and bags, and the yellow dog followed behind them.

"Can you tell me where Miss Mary Holden lives?" Mark asked a man on the porch of a store.

"In that white house up the hill," the man replied, pointing to a house that stood facing the river.

The old dread of meeting this great-aunt he scarcely knew came back to Mark. Footsteps in the dark, a washed-out bridge or a raging river were not to be feared as much as coming upon her like this, with six strangers and a cat and a dog. But he went up the hill and they all went with him.

In a garden, surrounded by a white fence, he saw an old lady dressed in black, with a white lace collar around her neck. A large white cat rubbed against her feet, and a spotted dog played close by. Now this was not the old lady, far back in his mem-

ory. Surely this was not the Great-Aunt Mary.

"Could you tell me where Miss Mary Holden lives?" he asked.

"I am Mary Holden, and I know you are Mark, for you are just like your father," the lady said, coming to meet him. Then she turned to the farmer and the two women and the three children. "Won't you come in, too, for it's a long time until the next bus leaves. It will be nice to have you wait here, for it has been lonesome living here alone." She led the way into the house where she prepared a hot breakfast.

"Long ago I had a housekeeper," she said, setting the plates on the long dining table. "But she was a fussy woman, screaming when a cat came near, hating dogs, and scolding when children made a noise. Now she's gone and I have a dog and a cat and all the children that want to come."

The Geography Lesson

Emma was awake and dressed while her sister Sara was still sound asleep, sunk deep in the feather bed. "Get up, Sara," she called, tugging at the quilt coverlet. "Mamma's got breakfast on the table, and I'm all ready for school."

Sara rubbed her eyes sleepily, then she picked up her clothes and ran to the warm kitchen to dress. "Even if you do have a head start," she said, pouring hot water from the kettle to the washbowl, "I can still get to school way yonder before you do."

It wasn't that Emma was slow. Whatever she did, she could be as quick about it as anyone. The trouble was she simply forgot to hurry when there was something else she was more interested in. Even now, when she should have been eating her breakfast, she was watching Taffy, the little red kitten, scamper about the floor, playing with an empty spool, crouching and pouncing and chasing it around in circles.

"Hurry, Emma," her mother said. "The new teacher's not going to like it if you go lagging in at the last minute when the bell's ringing."

Their father came in from the barnyard with a bucket of milk in each hand, and he set them on the kitchen bench to be strained, then he washed his hands and sat down at the table to join them. "I'd think an hour'd be plenty of time to make those two miles to school," he said.

"It would be for me if I didn't have Emma along," Sara said. "But I'm not going to wait for her this morning."

"When I was a young one, I had to go five miles, and if I was late, I was sure to catch a whipping," the father went on.

It was true that every morning, when the school bell rang, Emma was always the last of the line to march in. Often she had to run fast even to go in with the line at all. And of course it was always after sundown when she returned home. But the path to the school led through the forest, down the hill to the creek bottom, then up on another ridge, and there were so many things all along the way to catch the eye. Sometimes it was a rabbit crouching behind a stone the color of his fur, watching her every move with its round, dark eyes. And sometimes a squirrel scolded down from his perch high in a tree, or ants having a battle in the path before her.

Well now I'm ready ahead of time," Emma said, getting up from the table. She strapped her books together and picked up the tin bucket with the lunch of fried meat and biscuits and gingerbread her mother had fixed. Then she rushed outside, still buttoning her coat, and it was all Sara could do to keep up, at first.

"The capital of Mexico is Mexico City," Emma murmured to herself, with her eyes straight before her so she would not to be tempted to stop. "And it is bordered on the north by Texas, New Mexico, Arizona, and California."

Miss Dean, the teacher, had married and left, and now a new teacher was coming from town to take her place. It hadn't been easy to find one willing to come to a one-room school far out in a remote mountain settlement. And when one did, there was much talk, for everyone wondered what she was like. Would she be strict? And would she put on airs because she was from town, and laugh at their ways as visitors sometimes did?

The sun was just appearing over the eastern ridge when Emma and Sara started up the path through the woods. Spring comes early in the Arkansas Ozarks. The first little leaves were coming out on the red oaks and maples like red, velvety blossoms, and the elms catching the sun rays were pure gold against the dark green pines. It was such a short while ago that they were no more than tight little buds on the bare limbs. The ground was purple with wild violets and Emma and even Sara stopped to gather some for the new teacher.

"This is enough," Sara said, starting on her way again. "Come on, Emma, it's getting late."

Her bouquet was larger than Emma's, but she had not seen the little brown spotted quail sitting on her nest beneath the white oak tree. Emma hadn't dared call out for fear her voice would frighten the bird away. But it did not move, even at the sound of Sara's call and her footsteps passing by. Instead it seemed to merge and become part of the earth and rocks and dry, brown leaves. Emma blinked her eyes and looked hard before she found it again, though it had not moved so much as a feather.

Sara had already crossed the log at the creek and was on her way up the ridge when Emma tip-toed past the bird's nest. She stepped softly and carefully, trying to make no sound above the bird songs and the wind in the trees. A clump of cane grew in a circle near the creek, like a green, leafy wall around a small clearing. Something inside moved, and Emma stopped in her tracks, wondering what it could be. Her sister was already far ahead. She had almost reached the Johnson house on top of the ridge, and the Johnson twins were running out to join her.

"And it's bordered on the west by the Pacific Ocean and on the east by the Gulf of Mexico," Emma recited her geography lesson, as she started on to join her sister.

But when she reached the canebrake, there was a movement again inside. It wouldn't hurt to take one look, she thought, and then she'd run fast and reach the schoolhouse in time. She could hear her

sister's voice even now, though she was over the brow and out of sight. As quietly as a whisper of wind, Emma parted the cane stalks, and there in a little clearing she saw a doe with a new-born baby fawn lying beside her. The doe struggled to rise, but the little one only gazed at her with curiosity in its soft eyes. He was not at all afraid, and Emma was sure she was the first creature besides its mother that its eyes had ever looked upon.

The doe bent down her head and touched the fawn, and suddenly he looked up in alarm. Could the mother have been whispering to him, Emma wondered. She remained so still, with the gentle spring breeze blowing against her, so that the animals lost their fear. Emma didn't know how long she stood there. It seemed to her that she could see the strength come, bit by bit, to the fawn. He stood up on legs that were so spindly, they looked as if they would crack and splinter beneath his weight, and he nuzzled against his mother for milk. Then at last the two bounded off in the thickets as graceful as dancers.

Suddenly Emma realized that the sun was high over the ridge, and she no longer heard the voices of her sister and the Johnson twins. Now she must hurry. She crossed the log bridge and ran up the hill, over rocks and fallen logs, and around the big trees that grew in the path.

"The countries of Central America are Panama ... " Now what was the country lying north of Panama? It had gone completely from her mind. A dog came dashing out of the Johnson yard, wagging its tail and wanting to play, but Emma ran on without paying any attention to it. The schoolyard was

silent and empty. Could it be possible that the bell had rung and she didn't hear it? Emma hesitated before the door, dreading to enter, when suddenly it opened and she saw the pupils come marching out. There were twenty in all, from the oldest who was eighteen, to little Bess, five years old. And behind them came the teacher, wearing a green skirt and sweater, with her blond hair cut short.

It couldn't be recess, for no one ran off to play when the line was broken as they did at recess. And it couldn't be that school was out, for the sun hadn't gone to the west. Sara gave her a look of disapproval, but she didn't say anything.

"I'm sorry I'm late, ma'am," Emma began.

"You must be Emma Dixon, for that was the only name I called without an answer," the teacher said in a friendly voice. "Why were you late, Emma?" Emma told her then about the quail she had seen beneath the white oak tree, and the doe with her fawn in the cane thicket, and how she hadn't realized the time was passing as she stood watching them. The teacher frowned as she listened.

"The little fawn will have its lessons to learn, beginning even now," she said when Emma had finished. "It must learn the trails to the creek and to the salt licks. And it must learn which of the plants are good to eat and where the grass stays green longer in the autumn. And how to keep hidden from its enemies, the panther and wolf and the men who hunt it."

"And when the quails are hatched they'll have to learn how to be so still they'll look like the stones and dried leaves on the ground," Emma added.

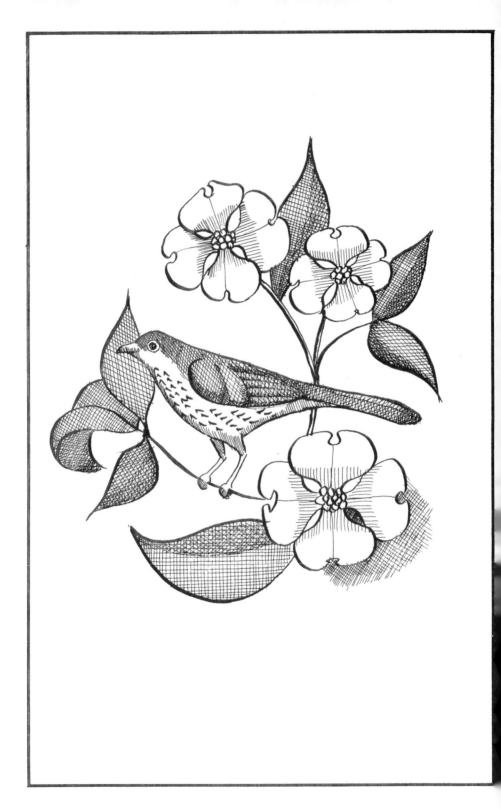

It came to her then that every living creature has lessons to learn. And her lessons were in the school as well as outside. She made up her mind then and there she'd never be late again.

"We're going on a field trip now for our nature study, and you may join us," the teacher said.

Emma didn't know quite what she meant until one of the Johnson twins pointed out the nest of a wood thrush in a dogwood tree. The teacher let them look, one by one, through the field glasses she had brought. When it was Emma's time, she held them to her eyes. Everything was blurred at first, until an older boy showed her how to turn the lenses until the bird in the nest seemed to be coming closer and closer. It looked then as if she could reach out her hand and touch it. The teacher was reading from a book, of how the nest was made of grass and bark strips and lined with fine rootlets of leaf mold. And she told of the countries where the wood thrush spent its winter, Mexico and Costa Rica.

Costa Rica! That was the name of the country north of Panama. Why, this was a geography lesson, too, that they were having, out here in the forest.

The Song

Janet Mitchell sat in her favorite place on the top step of the stair landing, with a writing pad across her knee, and a fountain pen in her hand. She had written "Dear Betty," but she could get no further. What could anyone say to Betty? Such interesting things were always happening to her, and her letter fairly bubbled over with news of them. Any kind of answer would be dull and drab in comparison.

Betty's father was an engineer and he was often sent to faraway places. And whenever he could, he took his family with him. Now he was in Europe, and Betty and her brother Jack had been allowed to go, too. Their parents had said they would learn more in a year of travel than in a schoolroom. But Janet's father was a doctor, and he stayed on in one place, seldom ever taking a vacation.

Betty's last letter had been from Venice, and Janet picked it up to read it again. But she knew it almost word for word from memory.

"It's just like the geography books said," she had written. "Songs and sunshine and lazy waters. This morning a gondola came right up to the door of the hotel for us, and we floated all over Venice in it. The gondolier stood in front of the boat while he paddled, and he sang such a gay song, Jack and I had to join in, though we didn't know a word we were singing. The pigeons at St. Mark's lit on our shoulders, begging for grain. And we saw a little old woman making the most beautiful lace you could ever imagine ..."

And so the letter went on and on. Janet drew idly on her writing pad.

"I received your letter from Venice," she began, then she paused again. There was simply no more to say. The day was gray and drizzling, and it had been over a week since the sun had been out. At school they had had to stay indoors during recess, for it was too wet and muddy to play outside. So there wasn't even a basketball game to write about. Janet saw her father coming down the stairs and she stood up to let him pass.

"Dad, they need doctors in Europe too, don't they?" she asked.

"Why, yes, of course. Doctors are very much needed over there," her father replied.

"Then why couldn't you be sent to some foreign country like Betty's father, and take Mother and little Helen and me?"

Doctor Mitchell smiled at the excitement in his daughter's eyes. But he shook his head and answered simply,"Doctors are needed here too, Janie."

He picked up his black doctor's bag from the hall table, and put on his raincoat and hat to go out on a call. But he stopped at the door and called back to Janet. "How'd you like to come along with me?"

Janet was all too eager for something to do on such a dismal Saturday. She rushed for her slicker and drew the hood snugly over her head, then followed her father to the garage. They took the jeep station wagon, which meant they were going far out in the country where the roads were rough and muddy.

"We'll have to hurry, for little Johnny Davis has had a fall from a grapevine on which he was swinging, and he's in pain."

The wind howled and the rain beat against the windshield so fast it was as if they were under a deep sea. And the tall trees along the roadside bowed and swayed and scattered their leaves in all directions. But the jeep station wagon pushed steadily ahead. They turned off the main highway, onto a narrow dirt road, passing through deep puddles and over rocks and ruts, and they crossed a bridge where the waters of the creek had risen so high, the waves lapped against the station wagon tires.

The river had risen too. Janet could hear its mighty roar, sounding above the wind in the trees and the falling rain. When the station wagon turned

and drove up to the top of the high levee, she could see the waves rushing swiftly along, carrying planks and tree branches and whatever had come within its reach.

They drove to a place where a horse and some cows were staked. The animals stopped nibbling the grass and looked up in curiosity, and there was a clatter of hens cackling in a coop and pigs squealing in a pen close by. Down in the valley below, a little farmhouse stood on high piers, surrounded on all sides by water. And a rowboat, tied to the porch rail, bobbed up and down with each splash of the waves.

"Here comes the doctor!" they heard a boy's voice call out excitedly. "Tell Johnny it's all right now. The doctor's come."

A man in overalls came out on the porch and, cupping his hands, shouted through them. "Leave your car there, doctor, I'll row over after you."

His arms moved swiftly with the oars, fighting against the strong current that tugged at the boat, as he wove in and out among the treetops that reached above the water.

"I'm glad you made it, doctor," he said when he pulled up at the levee. "We were afraid the high water would keep you from coming." He held the boat steady while Janet and her father stepped in, then he rowed back to the house as fast as he could. He pointed out a broken vine hanging from a tall pin oak growing close to the house. "Yonder's where he fell," he said. "Tried to act like Dan'l Boone and swing from the house to the barn without getting in the water."

Doctor Mitchell, with his black bag, went into a room where sounds could be heard of a child crying and a mother's voice trying to soothe and comfort him. Janet heard someone call to her from the kitchen. "Come in here, child, where it's warm."

She went in to find a little old woman sitting in a rocking chair near the stove. She was piecing gaily colored scraps of cloth to make a quilt. Two boys, older than Janet, were sitting beside her. One got up to bring in another chair and the other added more wood to the fire. A kettle on the stove began to bubble and sing, and a cat curled up on the floor beneath, purred in accompaniment. But a little mongrel puppy lay with its head on its front paws, looking with sad eyes toward the door where the sounds came from. The father came in and joined them, and they all sat silently, with their heads turned toward the room of the sick child.

"Now let's see what a brave boy you are, Johnny," they heard the doctor say. "Just a little more, and it'll all be over."

"Granny," the boy's father spoke in a low whisper, "sing the song Johnny always likes to hear, about the monkey's wedding."

"The monkey married the baboon's sister,
Gave her a ring and then he kissed her. ..."

The old woman's voice rose high and quavering. Her rocking chair kept time while she sang on to the end. And all the while her fingers were busy making dainty stitches, until the design of the quilt slowly began to take shape. When one song was ended, the woman began another one, and each was funnier and livelier than the last. The man and his two sons began stamping their feet to the rhythm, and joined their voices to hers. They sounded light and gay, but they glanced now and then with anxious eyes toward the door of the adjoining room.

"Chickens a crowin' on Sourwood Mountain
Ho ding, dong, doodle day.
So many pretty girls I can't count 'em"
Janet sang the last line with them:
"Ho ding, dong, doodle day."
The rain slackened and the sky began to clear. At last the sun shone through the parted clouds, sending its beams into the kitchen.

"My true love is a sun-burnt daisy . . . "
Now another voice joined them from the room beyond. The man and the two boys and the grandmother exchanged glances of relief, but they went on with the song, raising their voices even higher. And the mongrel puppy thumped his tail on the floor, happily.

"She won't work and I'm too lazy,
Ho ding, dong, doodle day."
The door opened, and Doctor Mitchell came out. "It's nothing more serious than a broken arm and a few bruises," he was saying. "He'll be as lively as ever in a couple of weeks if he promises not to swing on any more high grapevines."

The boy's mother smiled as she followed the doctor into the kitchen. And through the open door, Janet saw the boy himself, sitting up in bed and singing away for dear life.

Janet wondered, when she was again in the rowboat, going back to the levee, why she had ever found it hard to write a letter to Betty. Interesting things could happen anywhere. She had rowed in a boat right up the porch of a farmhouse. And she had seen a little old lady piecing a quilt with a design

more beautiful than anyone could imagine. But best of all, she had seen a boy smile and heard him join in a gay song because his pain had left him.

The Week of the Fair

It had been just a month since Elsie moved with her parents from the little town of Monticello to the big town of Little Rock. A month is a long time when you count it by the days. Thirty days to walk along the streets of the neighborhood, to see the people sitting on their porches late on a warm summer afternoon, and the children playing games in their front yards. At first there were nods, then cheerful greetings of "Good evening." Then there were visits, and hours of play with the girls her own age.

But Elsie thought of her friends back in Monticello, of Janet with her blue eyes and her yellow plaits down her back, and of chubby Mabel, with round, rosy cheeks.

She wanted to see them again, to tell them of all the things she had seen and done in the month she had lived in Little Rock, of the friendly old man next door who talked to his black cat as if it understood him, of Main Street, with its bright store windows and of the street around the corner, with girls and boys to play with, living in almost every house.

"Little Rock would be a nice place to live, if all the friends I like could come and live here, too," she said to her mother.

"In about two weeks from now the State Fair will be on. Why don't you write and invite your friends to come and visit you then," her mother suggested.

"I know they will come," Elsie said, and her eyes shone with excitement. "Janet and Mabel promised long ago they would come to the Fair when I first told them I was going to move here."

She ran to her room for pen and ink and paper, and brought them out on the porch. She sat on the steps to write her letters, where the light of late evening still lasted. It was much easier to think letters than it was to write them, for when she put pen to paper, she could think of nothing to say. At last she wrote:

"Dear Janet:

"We are going to have a State Fair in two weeks from now, and I wish you would come and visit me then. There will be horses and cows and pigs and a lady with snakes and a man that eats fire and

62

another that swallows swords, and merry-go-rounds to ride. I hope you can come.

> "Your friend,
> "Elsie Jackson.

> "P. S. — Tell your mother and father to come, too."

She wrote the same letter to Mabel. What fun it would be, roaming over Fair Park with Janet and Mabel, eating popcorn and candy, throwing hoops at a target, and looking at all the animals in their sheds. It would be still more fun if the Tucker girls could come, too. She would write and invite them. And there was the Harold boy. He had talked all last spring about the State Fair in Little Rock, and the calf he wanted to exhibit. Maybe if he had a place to stay, he could come and see it in its shed.

Now that she had started to write letters to her friends, it was like going back to Monticello for a visit. She must not forget old Mrs. Ragsdale, who lived all alone. She would enjoy a trip to Little Rock. And if she wrote Mrs. Ragsdale, she must write little Mrs. Brooks with the twins. And there was Janet's grandfather. He could not be left all alone.

Elsie used all her paper, then she wrote on sheets torn from her writing tablet. She wrote until she could no longer see by the fading light. Her mother called her in to her supper, and she stopped in the hall to put the letters in her father's brief case, so he could stamp and mail them.

The days passed, and there was talk everywhere of the coming State Fair. The newspapers

told of it in big black type, and there were advertisements on all the street cars and the buses, with pictures of a prize bull or a pig or fine vegetables heaped in a pile.

Elsie's mother made her a new blue dress to wear, and her father took her downtown to buy a pair of shoes and some blue socks to match her dress.

"Suppose they don't come," Elsie said.

"Oh, I'm sure Janet and Mabel will come. It's not so far for two little girls to travel on a bus," her mother replied.

Elsie made a wish on all the things that make a wish come true, on a falling star, on a load of hay that passed down the street, and on the wishbone of a chicken that she pulled under the table with her father. And her wish was always the same. "I wish my friends from Monticello would come and visit me during Fair Week."

On Sunday, the day before the opening of the Fair, Elsie was awake bright and early. She watched every cloud in the sky, and hoped it would pass over, and let the sun shine all during the week. Every time she heard footsteps on the sidewalk, or an automobile pass that way, she ran to the door to see who it was. And when she went to church school, she fidgeted and scarcely listened to the things the teacher said.

It was not until they sat down to their Sunday dinner that the doorbell rang for the first time. And there, with their two suitcases on the floor beside them, were Mr. and Mrs. Brooks, of Monticello, each holding a sleeping twin baby.

Elsie's mother hid the surprise she felt, and she

smiled as she welcomed them in and showed them the spare room. Then she set two more plates on the table.

"It was sweet of Elsie to write and invite us to come," Mrs. Brooks said when she joined them at the dinner table. "I've wanted a long time to go to the State Fair."

Scarcely had they finished their dinner, when the doorbell rang again. This time it was the Tucker girls with their mother and father.

"You can sleep on the living-room sofa," Elsie's mother whispered to Elsie. "We'll have to bring down the extra bed from the attic and put it in your room for them."

"I'd better sleep on a pallet and let Mrs. Ragsdale have the sofa," Elsie replied softly, for when she looked out the window she saw the old lady walking from the carline with her suitcase in her hand.

"I vow I never would have dreamed of coming in to Little Rock if this dear child hadn't invited me to," she said, a little breathless from her walk.

The Harold boy came next, and then an automobile drove up to the gate, and out stepped Mabel, and her jolly fat father, and her equally jolly, fat mother.

"Elsie," her mother said, when they were alone at last, washing and drying the supper dishes, "when I said you might write and invite your friends to come and visit you when the State Fair was on, how many did you invite?"

"There's still Janet and her mother and father and grandfather," Elsie replied.

Mrs. Jackson sighed. And then she laughed.

"I think I understand," she said, and she bent

down to kiss the troubled look from Elsie's face. "I've been homesick, too, for all the friends we left behind, and I've wanted to be with them, though I didn't expect them all at the same time. But, we'll manage, somehow."

Mattresses and pallets of patchwork quilts were spread on the floors of every room in the house, even in the dining room and kitchen. And when Janet, with her parents and grandfather, came late that night, still more pallets were put down. Six little letters to write and send off had not seemed many to Elsie. But when they brought such a crowd of people here, it was as though the whole town of Monticello had been moved into this little white house in Little Rock.

Elsie tried to count them, but she gave it up, for they were moving in and out of the rooms so fast that some were counted twice and some were not counted at all. "Maybe it's better to have only one friend at a time," she thought.

But early the next morning she was awakened by the sound of the women moving quietly about, making beds, sweeping floors, cooking breakfast, and setting the table. And before she could blink her eyes fully awake, she was called in to breakfast with the other children.

"And now, when you have finished eating, put on your prettiest dresses, for we will all go to the Fair together," said Mabel's fat, jolly mother.

Some went in automobiles, some on the street car, and some went on the motorbus. Elsie wore her new blue dress and her blue socks to match, and she sat in Mabel's lap, in Mabel's father's automobile. Zip, the Airedale puppy, whined and wanted to go, too. He ran after the automobile for a little way, then gave it up and turned back to keep watch over the house, while everyone was away.

Elsie and Janet and Mabel and the Harold boy and the Tucker girls kept close together. With a colored balloon in one hand and a hot dog, dripping with mustard and pickles, in the other, they explored every nook and corner of the great Fair Park, from the shed where the fattest and sleekest of pigs were kept, to the counters of cotton bolls and squash and turnips as big as a man's head.

"Step this way, folks, and see the strangest show on earth!" a man called from one side.

"Right over here, folks! Take a ride on the Ferriswheel," a man called from the other side.

I've never had so much fun in all my life," Mabel said, taking a bite of pink cotton candy.

"And we couldn't have come if you hadn't asked us," Janet joined in.

They did not know that they were tired until they had returned home that night. But even then, no one was ready to go to sleep except the twin babies. They slept peacefully on, in a house made merry by the sound of talk and laughter of friends meeting after a long absence. They sat in the parlor and on the porch, and even on the banisters and the porch steps.

The man next door came over to join them. He talked of old times in Little Rock, and Janet's grandfather talked of old times in Monticello. And the tales they told were much the same, of medicine shows on street corners, and of serenaders with banjos and guitars going from house to house to play their music. As Elsie listened, the thought came

to her that some day, this, too, would be old times. Some day the State Fair with the fat, sleek pigs and the pink cotton candy and the gypsy fortuneteller would be only things to tell about. Even now the music of the merry-go-round was still in her ears, and the sight of the crowds still moved in her mind.

"Next summer when we have the Home Coming Week in Monticello, be sure and come to stay with us," Mrs. Brooks said.

"I want you to stay with me," Janet said to Elsie.

"And I want you with me," Mabel said.

And Elsie knew that she would be made welcome in every home in Monticello.

New Friends

The light of early morning came through the window, pale gray at first, to mingle with the dark shadows of the room. Then it turned to red and orange, coloring the bureau and the chair, and reflecting itself in the mirror on the wall. A cardinal on a hickory tree chirped softly as a sleepy child might answer when his mother called to wake him up in the morning.

"It's no different from home," Elsie thought.

She searched the bureau drawer for her starched gingham dress, and then she searched for

her shoes and her socks. Everything was topsy-turvy in a house just moved into.

"Back home in Monticello, there was a hickory tree close to my window, where a red bird built its nest," she said, half-singing it to herself.

But she must not think of Monticello as home any more. Little Rock was her home now. Only last night she had watched the empty moving van go off into darkness on its way back to Monticello. Little Rock had meant no more to her than a strange house filled with packing boxes, and their furniture scattered about in unaccustomed places. But now that morning had come, there was a whole new world before her, waiting to be explored.

"Little Rock is fifty times bigger than Monticello, with fifty times more people in it," her father said at the breakfast table.

Elsie thought of the little town they had left, with its park where the band concert played in the summer, and the stores on the four streets all around it. She knew everybody there, and she knew each time a stranger came to town. Would anyone know that she was a stranger, come to live in Little Rock? There had been fifteen pupils in her class at school there. In her head she multiplied them by fifty. Seven hundred and fifty classmates! And would there be a hundred best friends like Janet and Mabel, who lived on her street in Monticello? It made her head swim to think about it.

Before she finished her breakfast, with a piece of bread and jam still in her hand, she went out the front door and down the street, but it was like any other street, with quiet little houses standing in a row. There were the same grassy yards and the

same late marigolds and asters blooming in them. And there were no more people walking along the sidewalks than there were in Monticello on a week day morning. A man passed by on his way to work, with his lips moving as if he were talking to himself, and a woman across the street came out to sweep her porch. But there was no sign of children any-where.

There were faces in the windows of the houses next door, but they did not look her way. On one side a woman sat near the light, reading her morning paper. And on the other side, an old man with white hair and a white mustache watered pink petunias that grew in a window box.

From far away there came a shout as of children at play, but the street was so quiet, she was sure she must have been mistaken. It may have been a bird, fully awake now and calling out, or it may have been a dog yelping in fright. Where were all these people, fifty times as many as there were in Monticello?

Zip, the Airedale puppy, lay down on the grass beside her, tired now from sniffing all the unfamiliar smells. He bit off a blade of grass and spit it out again. Then he raised his head and sniffed the air, quivering. Soon a black cat walked out on the porch of the house where the old man was watering his petunias. Zip went dashing off, under the fence and on to the neighbor's porch.

"Come back, Zip!" Elsie called, but the dog did not pay any attention. The cat had scurried high up in a redbud tree, and the dog stayed below, wagging his tail at the thought of a fight with a cat.

"I'd be ashamed," Elsie said, picking the dog up and taking him into the house. But Zip only wagged his tail.

Elsie went back into the yard next door to try to coax the black cat down, but the cat only climbed higher, mewing miserably.

Where there was a cat, there must surely be some young people, Elsie thought. She looked toward the door, half-expecting to see a girl with blue eyes and yellow plaits down her back, like Janet, or a chubby girl with round, rosy cheeks, like Mable in Monticello. But instead, the little old man came out and walked to the redbud tree. He reached out his hand, and slowly the cat backed down, stopping now and then to see if the hand were still there. Then she gave a leap and landed on the man's shoulder.

"I'm glad you remembered what I told you about coming down a tree exactly the way you go up, with your back to the ground so you can dig your claws in," he said, and he went into the house, still talking as if the cat could understand what he said.

He came out again soon after, with a straw hat on and a bamboo cane in his hand.

"Good morning," he said to Elsie, as if seeing her for the first time. "I'm going calling on some old friends, this morning. Would you like to come with me?"

He had scarcely spoken the words when Elsie ran into the house for her mother's consent and ran out again, wearing her wide straw hat with streamer down the back. Zip followed behind, looking back now and then at the window where the black cat sat watching them.

The old man took short little steps, using his

cane to help him, and Elsie walked slowly beside him.

"Back home," she started, then she caught herself and said, "In Monticello, where I used to live, strangers didn't go out to make the first calls. The folks went to call on them instead, to welcome them to town."

"The ones we are calling on can't come to welcome you, for they are trees," the old man replied.

Elsie looked up to see if he were joking, but he went on, calmly. "When I was a boy, Little Rock was only a small town, about the size your Monticello is now, and I knew everybody in it. We boys used to play every day by the town creek, before it was closed over. We climbed the trees that grew along the banks, and we tied stout ropes in them to make swings, and we jumped from their branches for a swim when the water was up, or hid behind them when we fought make-believe Indians with our bows and arrows. Now the boys are all gone, but the trees are still here, just the same, never changing. Every season I come to make them a call, when their leaves are new in the spring, when they are fully out in all their summer foliage, and in the autumn when the leaves are turning and ready to fall, and in the winter, when the leaves are bare and the trees are half-asleep. They are the only friends I have left, now."

"Where did the boys go that you played with when you were little?" Elsie asked.

"Some went away to bigger cities, some died, some moved to another part of town, and some forgot they were ever small boys, for they were so busy making money."

They turned down one street and then another, and while the old man's walk was slow, they went far that morning. First they stopped before a great white oak that stood close to the sidewalk in a small yard.

"This old tree was as big as it is now, even when I was a boy," the old man said. "We tied a rope swing to that high branch yonder, and when we were in it, we could see far over the roof tops of Little Rock."

Elsie tried to think of this old man beside her, as a small boy, playing with other boys, swinging high in the tree long ago.

"This one is a stubborn tree," the old man went on. "It holds to its leaves and will not let them go as the other trees do. It keeps them all winter, dry and brown, until the new little green leaves push them off in the spring."

"And when the new leaves of the white oak are the size of a mouse's ear, then there will be no more frost," Elsie said.

"Yes, the Indians knew long ago when to plant their corn by the size of this old tree's leaves."

They walked on, turning down one street after another until they came to a tall cypress. It grew close to the red brick wall of an apartment house and towered above it, shading the windows from the south sun with its branches. The leaves were turning a rusty brown, ready to fall for the winter.

"This is where the town creek ran," the old man said.

"Did the cypress have little knees coming out of the water?" Elsie asked, remembering the cypress swamps that grew close to her old home.

"Yes, like little gnomes caught in their play and turned to wood." he replied.

Now the gnomelike knees and the trickling creek were covered with a cement sidewalk and a black paved street with buses and street cars running over it.

The old man told of how the cypress grew, from a tiny seed dropped from another tree long ago, when only Indians and wild animals of the forest roamed the land. He told of the Spaniards that stopped under it to rest when they came here looking for gold, and of the French who came to explore, and then of the early settlers who built their log cabins near the shade of the tree.

"The creek still runs along here," he said as they walked on, their steps keeping time to the tap of his cane upon the cement walk, and the little dog trotted behind. Elsie knew that underneath where she walked, and underneath the street where automobiles passed to and fro, a creek of water flowed on its way to the river. They stopped before a holly tree with green berries forming that would turn bright red when the cold weather came, to be used for Christmas decorations. At each tree little Zip sniffed, wanting to know it, too, and Elsie looked up at it as if it were a new friend, welcoming her to her new home. They came to a pecan tree with its green pods parting and the brown nuts already peeping from their downy nests.

"I planted this tree myself," the man said. He told of how he had watched a squirrel burying acorns in the ground, and he took the nut from his pocket and put it in the hole, too, when the squirrel had gone.

"The squirrel either forgot or smelled the touch of my hand, for the next year a little oak and a little pecan seedling grew up from the ground. I pulled up the oak and let the pecan grow, watching it every year from a thin sapling to the big tree you see here."

They turned another corner and they came to a vacant lot, where a tall persimmon tree grew, with its ladder-like branches growing over the roofs of the houses around it. And under the tree a crowd of children played, more than there were in all of Monticello, Elsie was sure. Some were swinging high in swings and some were pushing them. Some played on a see-saw and some played jacks and ball near its shade. And two little girls were keeping house beside it, with lines drawn in the earth to mark the rooms, and the leafy branches making a roof over their heads. The persimmons clung to the tree with their little dark caps, waiting for the cold frost to make them soft and sweet to taste.

"Where the great trees are, you generally find children," said the old man, and smiled wisely.

"Hello," a girl Elsie's own age called out to her.

"Hello," Elsie replied, and Zip wagged his tail in greeting, too.

"Come and play with us," the girl said. "You can swing next in the swing."

Elsie looked around the corner of the vacant lot, and saw that it was her own street, with her own white house on it.

"I can't now, but I'll come back later," she called, and, walking beside the old man, she waved to the girl, who waved in reply and smiled a friendly smile.